THE
KINGDOM
OF MINE

Text and illustrations © 2012 by Garold Edwards

Published in the United States by Cupola Press®

www.cupolapress.com

Library of Congress Control Number: 2011907320

ISBN-13: 978-0-9834046-1-3

First Edition   10 9 8 7 6 5 4 3 2 1

Printed in Singapore

The Kingdom of Mine

By Gary Edwards

Illustrated By Masako Dunn

Cupola
PRESS®

LAFAYETTE, CALIFORNIA

I know of a place not far from here where the land is littered with rocks. Mile after mile of stone — small rocks and large boulders. Most people think this is a natural phenomenon, but I know differently. Let me tell you the story about the rocks in the meadow…

Contents

Many years ago there was a small kingdom ruled by a very good king. He loved his people and his land, and the people loved their king.

It was a beautiful land with rich, green grass. Natural springs bubbled with fresh, clean water. The springs fed a small river that brought the pure water to the people, and the cows that grazed by the river provided the sweetest milk. When the days were cool, the bright sun warmed the land, and when the days were hot, soft breezes cooled the air. At night, the stars shone bright and clear.

The king had a son who grew up to be a strong and handsome prince. The prince learned everything he could from his father, for he knew that some day he would be king.

When the old king died, the people in the kingdom were very sad, but they knew the strong, young prince would become their king, and that comforted them.

On the day the prince was crowned king, the people threw a great party. Under a bright sun in a beautiful meadow, with a fresh breeze blowing, they crowned the prince their new king. They celebrated with a wonderful feast of wholesome foods grown in the kingdom.

The young king promised to carry on the legacy of his father and to protect all that his father had cherished in the land. He promised to watch over the people and the land with kindness and respect.

And the people were pleased.

Apples

The young king enjoyed walking, and he liked to pick apples from a tree near the border of the neighboring kingdom. The apples from that tree were the most wonderful in the land, both sweet and tart, and so full of flavor that the juice would run down his face when he took a bite.

One day as the king was walking, he noticed a group of children from the neighboring kingdom picking apples from his favorite tree.

He called to the children, "What are you doing here? Don't you know this tree is not yours?"

The children replied, "We're sorry, but we didn't know that anyone owned this tree. The apples look so good — we only wanted to taste them."

"Well!" said the king. "I think you should leave my kingdom, go back to your own land, and stay away from my apples! Please do not come here again."

The children were very sad as they left.

The king was sad, too. "But," he thought, "this is my land and these are my apples. I must protect the things that are mine." He wondered, though, how the children could know that this was his land.

Then he had an idea: "I shall build a small fence and put up signs to tell people that this is my kingdom. Then they will know they shouldn't come over the fence to pick the apples, for they are mine."

So he called together his royal architects and builders. The boundaries were mapped, and they designed and built a low fence. The fence was made of stone collected from the meadow. All around the fence, signs were posted that said: "THIS KINGDOM IS MINE. PLEASE LEAVE IT ALONE."

When the building was finished, the king looked at his fence and felt good, knowing his apples would never be taken again.

Deer

One day as the king was walking, he noticed some deer grazing on the sweet, green grass near the river. The king had always loved the deer, and it pleased him to see them.

Suddenly, one of the deer kicked up his heels in fun and ran toward the low fence the king had built. The deer easily jumped over the fence, and the rest of the deer followed.

"Why!" the king exclaimed. "Those are my deer! They have left my land to go into the neighboring kingdom, and they may not come back. What am I to do?"

Then he said to himself, "I know. I will make the fence higher to keep in the animals. Then they will know they shouldn't leave this place, for they are mine."

So he called together his royal architects and builders, and the stone fence was made higher — high enough to keep the strongest deer from jumping over. When the building was finished, the king looked at his fence and felt good, knowing his deer and all the other animals in his kingdom could never leave.

Birds

One day as the king was walking, he noticed birds singing beautiful songs in a tree above him. The king had always loved birds, and it pleased him to listen to them.

Suddenly the whole flock of birds flew out of the tree and high into the sky. The king watched with dismay as he saw the birds fly into the neighboring valley and alight upon a distant field.

"Why!" the king exclaimed. "Those are my birds! They have left my land to go into the neighboring kingdom, and they may not come back. What am I to do?"

"I know," he thought. "I will make the fence higher to keep in the birds. Then they will know they shouldn't leave this place, for they are mine."

So he called together his royal architects and builders. And the stone fence was made higher until it became a wall — a wall so high that even the strongest eagle couldn't escape.

When the building was finished, the king looked at his wall and felt good, knowing the birds in his kingdom could never leave.

Clouds

One day as the king was walking, he noticed a beautiful cloud in the sky. The king had always loved the clouds, and it pleased him to see them.

Suddenly a gust of wind blew the cloud away from the kingdom into the neighboring valley, where its gentle rain watered the trees and flowers.

"Why!" the king exclaimed. "That was my cloud and my rain! It has left my land to go into the neighboring kingdom, and it may not come back. What am I to do?"

"I know," he thought. "I will make the wall higher to keep in the clouds. Then they will know they should not leave this place, for they are mine."

So he called together his royal architects and builders. The designs were drawn, and the stone wall was made higher, so high it reached into the sky.

And just as the wall was being finished, a few clouds came in on a gust of wind and were trapped inside the wall of the kingdom. When the building was finished, the king looked at his wall and felt good, knowing the beautiful clouds in his kingdom could never leave.

Changes

After a while, the king began to see changes taking place in his kingdom. It seemed as if a great sadness had come across the land and his people. The king noticed a change in himself, too, for the things that used to please him weren't as pleasant anymore. The sun didn't seem so bright, the grass wasn't quite so green, and the water was no longer clean and pure.

This bothered the king, so he did what he had always done to raise his spirits — he went for a walk in his kingdom.

First he went to his favorite apple tree. But when the king walked up to the tree, he found that the apples were no longer juicy and sweet. The wall the king had built blocked the sunshine, so the few apples that grew on the tree were small, wrinkled, and blotchy in color. Before the apples had a chance to ripen, they would rot and fall to the ground.

This made the king very sad.

When the king was sad, it always raised his spirits to see the deer, so he went to look for them.

But when the king found the deer, he noticed they no longer ran and kicked up their heels. Since they could not jump over the wall, they spent most of their days standing or walking alongside it. Their coats, which had once been shiny and sleek, were now dusty and dingy. Worst of all, they did not hold their heads up high. In fact, it seemed to the king that they were not happy at all.

And this made the king very sad.

When the king was sad, it always raised his spirits to watch the birds fly and to hear them sing, so he went to look for them.

But when the king found the birds, he did not hear them singing or see them flying. Since they could not fly high enough to go over the wall and explore, they merely walked around, pecking at the ground.

This made the king very sad.

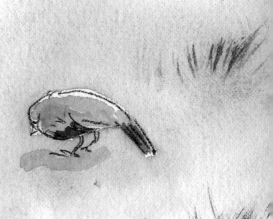

When the king was sad, it always raised his spirits to lie on the sweet, green grass and watch the clouds as they floated across the sky, so he looked for a special place to lie down.

But when the king looked for a special place, he found that the grass was not green and sweet. In some places it was brown and dry, and in other places it was damp and black with mold. So the king simply stood where he was and looked up at the sky, hoping to find a beautiful cloud to lift his spirits.

But when the king looked up to the sky, he saw just one tiny, tired cloud. This was all that was left of the beautiful clouds that had entered his kingdom just as the wall was completed. As the king looked up, the last cloud cried a few drops of rain onto the land…then disappeared.

Now the young king was sadder than he had ever been since his father, the old king, had died. And he wondered what had changed.

Then he thought about the apple tree and how the children from the neighboring kingdom had eaten the juicy, sweet apples. He thought about the low fence he had ordered to be built. "But I was only trying to protect what was mine," he thought.

Then he considered the deer and how they jumped over the fence and ran into the neighboring valley. And he thought about how he had ordered the fence to be raised. "But I was only trying to protect what was mine," he thought.

Then he thought about the birds and the clouds and about the fence he had ordered to be built into a wall that reached to the sky.

And then he had a different thought…

The Awakening

"Perhaps these things aren't really mine after all. Perhaps they never *were* mine. My father, the old king, never needed a fence to keep children from the apple tree. That tree grew the best apples in the land, and yet there were always more apples than I could eat.

"The deer, before the fence was built higher, used to run and play in this valley and the next. They were happy and healthy, and it pleased us all to see them.

"The birds used to sing in the sunshine and fly in the fresh air. Now the sun hides behind the wall, and the birds hardly ever sing or fly.

"The clouds I loved so much have disappeared, and not even the strongest wind can blow more clouds over the wall. I have tried so hard to protect what I thought was mine. But now I see I have nearly destroyed everything that is important to me."

The Plan

So the king came up with a new plan. He asked all of the people of his kingdom to gather together for a great meeting.

The people came from near and far. They had not been together since he was crowned king, a happy time for all. But this time when the people gathered, the king saw that no one was smiling.

When the king began to speak, the people noticed a change in him. He seemed humble, and he no longer acted as if he had all the answers. The first words out of the king's mouth surprised the people more than anything else he could have said.

The king said, "I'm sorry."

The people started whispering among themselves. Did he really say he was sorry?

And the king continued...

"As your king, I promised to take care of all you entrusted to me. But after a while, I began to believe that all things in this kingdom were mine: the apples on the tree, the deer in the meadows, the birds in the sky, even the sky itself. But those were foolish thoughts. The trees were here before I was born, and the deer are meant to be free. The birds in the sky and the sky itself aren't mine — they do not belong to any one of us. We are meant to watch over and protect them, but we are not to contain them, for to contain them may destroy them, as I have nearly destroyed our beautiful kingdom.

"But," the king continued, "there is always hope, and hope with action can bring change. The change I propose is to restore this land to the beauty and fullness we enjoyed when my father was king."

With that comment, the king began to climb the stone wall he had ordered to be built. The people watched him as he climbed higher and higher until they could barely see him. At last he stood on top of the wall. Then he bent down and pried loose a large stone and hurled it over the wall. Then he pried loose another and another. The people looked on in amazement as the king worked furiously to undo the wrong he had done to them and to the land.

A great cheer went up from the people as a gust of fresh air passed through the opening the king had made in the wall. Then the people began to climb the wall to join the king at the top. Everyone helped cast stones, big ones and small ones, over the wall. As fresh air blew into the kingdom, the spirits of the people were raised.

With all the excitement, the birds began to fly around to find out what was happening. The birds were so delighted to be able, once again, to see over the wall, they started singing the most beautiful songs ever heard. As the songs of the birds floated through the kingdom, the spirits of the people were raised.

When the wall was lower still, the deer began to notice the commotion. One deer kicked up her heels and jumped on top of the wall, then disappeared to the other side. Then she returned, jumping on top and over the wall again, calling for her friends to join her. As the deer kicked up their heels, jumping back and forth over the wall, the spirits of the people were raised.

Finally, as the wall became a low fence, the sun shone on the king's favorite apple tree. The tree

had been in shade for so long that no one expected
it to ever produce fruit again. But as the wall came
down and fresh air blew into the kingdom, as the
birds flew and the deer kicked up their heels, and as
the sun shone on the apple tree, a marvelous thing
happened…a small blossom opened on the tree.
Then another and another. And the tree came into
full bloom – full with the promise of tomorrow.

And a great joy spread across the land.

The Resolution

After the wall came down, the king found that the things that used to please him were pleasant again, but the land surrounding the kingdom was littered with the stone that had been used in its construction. The people asked the king what should be done with it. Should it be put into piles or carted off? Should it be hidden to put the sad days of the wall behind them?

But the king, now older and wiser, said, "No. The stone comes from this land, and it belongs here. Let us leave it where it has fallen so we never forget the lessons we have learned. Nature is here for all of us to enjoy, and we share a responsibility to care for it wisely. If we don't act in harmony with nature, we don't know what might happen in the future. Let us be thoughtful and careful in our actions, so the trees and animals and birds may be enjoyed by everyone, today and forever."

The people listened and were happy, for once again the kingdom was a beautiful land with rich, green grass. Natural springs bubbled with fresh, clean water. The springs fed a small river that brought the pure water to the people, and the cows that grazed by the river provided the sweetest milk. When the days were cool, the bright sun warmed the land, and when the days were hot, soft breezes cooled the air. At night the stars shone bright and clear.

And the people from the kingdom, their children, and their grandchildren learned to tell the story of the rocks in the meadow, and we have learned from them. Now we tell the story to our children so that you, too, may learn and never forget.